For Thomas Owlett
who introduced his bucketful of dinosaurs
to Ann and me one lucky Sunday afternoon
at The Chelsea Gardener
I.W.

For William
A.R.

With thanks to Dr Angela Milner
at the Natural History Museum, London

First published in Great Britain in 1999
by David & Charles Children's Books
Published in this edition in 2001 by

GULLANE
CHILDREN'S BOOKS

Winchester House, 259-269 Old Marylebone Road,
London NW1 5XJ

3 5 7 9 10 8 6 4

Text © Ian Whybrow 1999
Illustrations © Adrian Reynolds 1999

A CIP record for this title is available from the British Library.

ISBN 1 86233 338 6 (this edition)
ISBN 1 86233 088 3 (standard size hardback)
ISBN 1 86233 205 3 (standard size paperback)
ISBN 1 86233 227 4 (gift pack)

Manufactured in China

Harry
and the
Bucketful of
Dinosaurs

Written by Ian Whybrow
Illustrated by Adrian Reynolds

GULLANE
CHILDREN'S BOOKS

Nan thought the attic needed a clear out.
She let Harry help.
Harry found an old box
all grey with dust.

He lifted the lid . . .
DINOSAURS!

Harry took the
dinosaurs downstairs.

He unbent the
bent ones.

He fixed all the
broken ones.

He got up on a chair and washed them in the sink.
Nan came to see and say, "Just what do
you think you're up to?"

"Dinosaurs don't like boxes," Harry said.
"They want to be in a bucket."

Sam came in from watching TV.
She said it was stupid, fussing over so much junk.
"Dinosaurs *aren't* junk," Harry said.

The next day, Harry went to the library with Mum.
He took the dinosaurs in their bucket.

He found out all the names in a book
and told them to the dinosaurs.
He spoke softly to each one.
He whispered,
　　"*You are my Scelidosaurus.*"
　　　"*You are my Stegosaurus.*"
　　　　"*You are my Triceratops.*"

And there were enough names for all the Apatosauruses
and Anchisauruses and Tyrannosauruses.
The dinosaurs said, "Thank you, Harry."
They said it very quietly, but just
loud enough for Harry to hear.

After that, the dinosaurs went everywhere in Harry's bucket.

They went shopping.

They went to the garden centre.

Sometimes they got left behind.
But they never got lost for long because
Harry knew all their names.

And he always called out their names,
just to make sure they were safe.

One day, Harry went on a train with Nan.
He was so excited, he forgot all
about the bucket.

Nan dried his eyes.
"Never mind," she said.
"I'll buy you a nice new video."

Harry watched the video with Sam.
It was nice, but not like the dinosaurs.

At bedtime, Harry said to Mum, "I like videos.
But I like my dinosaurs better
because you can fix them, you can bath them,
you can take them to bed.

And best of all, you can say their names."

Harry was still upset at breakfast next morning.
Sam said, "*Dusty old junk!*"
That was why Sam's book got milk on it.
Nan took Harry to his room to settle down.

Later, Nan took Harry back to the train station to
see the Lost Property Man.
The man said, "Dinosaurs? Yes we have found some dinosaurs.
But how do we know they are *your* dinosaurs?"

Harry said, "I will close
my eyes and call their names.
Then you will know."

And Harry closed his eyes and called the names.
He called,

"Come back

my Scelidosaurus!"

"Come back my Stegosaurus!"

"Come back my Triceratops!"

He called, 'come back', to the Apatosauruses
  and the Anchisauruses
  and the Tyrannosauruses
  and all the lost old dinosaurs.
And when he opened his eyes . . .

. . . there they were – all of them standing on
the counter next to the bucket!
"All correct!" said the man.
"These are *definitely* your dinosaurs. Definitely!"

And the dinosaurs whispered to Harry.
They whispered very quietly, but
just loud enough for Harry to hear.
They said, "You are definitely *our* Harry, definitely!"

Going home from the station,
Harry held the bucket very tight.
Nan said to the neighbour, "Our Harry
likes those old dinosaurs."

"Definitely," whispered Harry.
"And my dinosaurs definitely like me!"

ENDOSAURUS

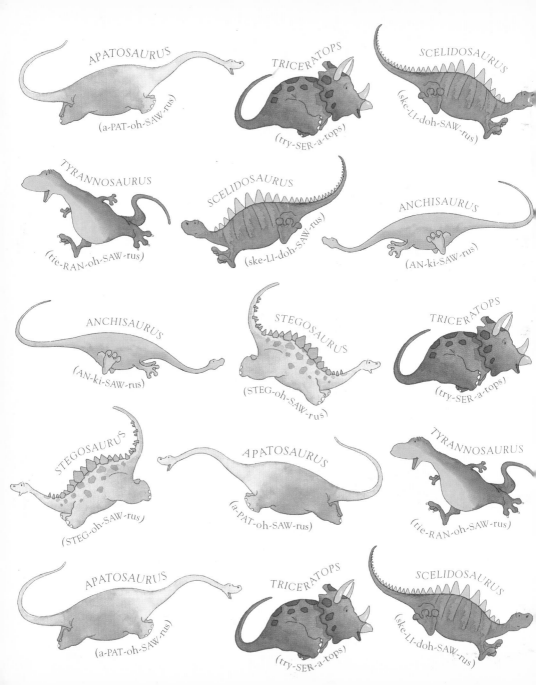